LONE WOLF and CUB

by
KAZUO KOIKE
and
GOSEKI KOJIMA

cover by
FRANK MILLER
and
LYNN VARLEY

子連れ狼

第1巻

小池一夫
小島剛夕

FIRST PUBLISHING

AF799500

Kazuo Koike
STORY

Goseki Kojima
ART

Frank Miller
COVER ILLUSTRATION & INTRODUCTION

Christine Miyuki Martine and Alex Wald
ENGLISH ADAPTATION

Willie Schubert
LETTERING

Paul Guinan
PRODUCTION

Rick Oliver
EDITOR

Rick Obadiah
PUBLISHER

Alex Wald
ART DIRECTOR

Kathy Kotsivas
OPERATIONS DIRECTOR

Rick Taylor
PRODUCTION MANAGER

Kurt Goldzung
SALES DIRECTOR

Lone Wolf and Cub (Kozure Okami) © 1987 Kazuo Koike and Goseki Kojima.

English translation © 1987 First Comics, Inc. and Global Communications Corporation.

Cover illustration and introduction © 1987 Frank Miller.

Published monthly in the United States of America by First Comics, Inc., 435 N. LaSalle, Chicago Il 60610, and Studio Ship, Inc. under exclusive license by Global Communications Corporation, Musashiya Building, 4th Floor, 27-10, Aobadai 1-Chome, Meguro-Ku, Tokyo, 153 Japan, owner of world wide publishing rights to the property Lone Wolf and Cub.

Lone Wolf and Cub #2 (ISBN 0-915419-11-4) © 1987 First Comics, Inc. and Global Communications Corporation. All rights reserved.

First printing, June 1987
Second printing, June 1987

INTRODUCTION

If you love comic books, you're well aware of the problem we face in getting the civilian population to take us seriously. A number of people in the field think the term "comic book" itself is at the heart of our difficulty, grouping us with Saturday morning cartoons and Transformers robots and declaring to the world at large that we offer nothing you wouldn't trust to come out of a Pez dispenser. "Serious comic" sounds, to most, like a contradiction in terms.

In recent years, the more respectable sounding title of "graphic novel" has begun to catch on. Unfortunately, it's been used almost exclusively as a designation of format, rather than content, indicating that the comic is printed on glossy paper with painted color as a trade paperback. But the novel, in prose, is an established literary form, larger and greater in scope than the short story. A graphic novel, if the term is going to mean anything more than "deluxe format" or "Baxter book," should be as rich in texture and full of story as its prose counterpart.

First Publishing's release of Kazuo Koike's and Goseki Kojima's graphic novel, Lone Wolf and Cub, is well-timed. We've just now figured out what to call it. Lone Wolf is a full-fledged adventure novel, in the grand sense. It takes you to another time, and to a frightening, alien land, windswept and grey, dying in quiet obedience to the insane decrees of insane leaders. Its authors took the time and space to tell their tale in its every moment, often devoting many pages to scenes that wouldn't last three panels in a monthly American superhero comic book. We come to know the players, large and small, as we meet them, as they reveal themselves to us. Koike and Kojima tell their story masterfully and artfully, portraying a man, a boy, and a country on their journey into Hell.

This segment features the plight of a lowly maid, and her encounter with a samurai warrior who's still a few years short of puberty.

And many other things.

—*Frank Miller*
Los Angeles, 1987

序文

PROLOG

Wrongfully accused of plotting to overthrow the Shogun, **Itto Ogami** becomes an outlaw, wandering through the provinces of feudal Japan with his infant son **Daigoro** by his side, seeking vengeance for the murder of his wife and family.

Ogami survives by his wits — and frequently by offering his services as a paid assassin. Sometimes his victims deserve the death he coldly metes out; other times they do not. But either way, Ogami is utterly committed to his task if he accepts payment and gives his word of honor. That is the way of the Samurai.

Once Ogami had been the Shogun's official executioner, using his deft swordmanship to end the lives of rebellious lords who defied the Shogun. His skills with the blade were legendary.

Ogami is feared by many in powerful places. They fear unseen enemies; they fear revenge from the families of those they murdered to attain their positions; they fear the Lone Wolf. They would kill Ogami before he has a chance to strike if they did not have to face his deadly blade. Now the Lone Wolf lies unconscious, deathly ill. Now he is defenseless. Now they will come. Now only the infant Daigoro — the Lone Wolf's cub — stands between his father and an army of assassins determined to destroy the Lone Wolf.

序文

お末無情
其之三
PITIFUL OSUE

RUSTLE
IS THIS YOUR KITE, LITTLE BOY?
NOPE.

OSUE! GET OVER HERE!
RUSTLE
HEY, THAT'S MY KITE!
YOU LITTLE THIEF!

SMACK!
YAAH!
OW!
AAIIEEEE!
YOU LITTLE BRAT!
HOW DARE YOU!

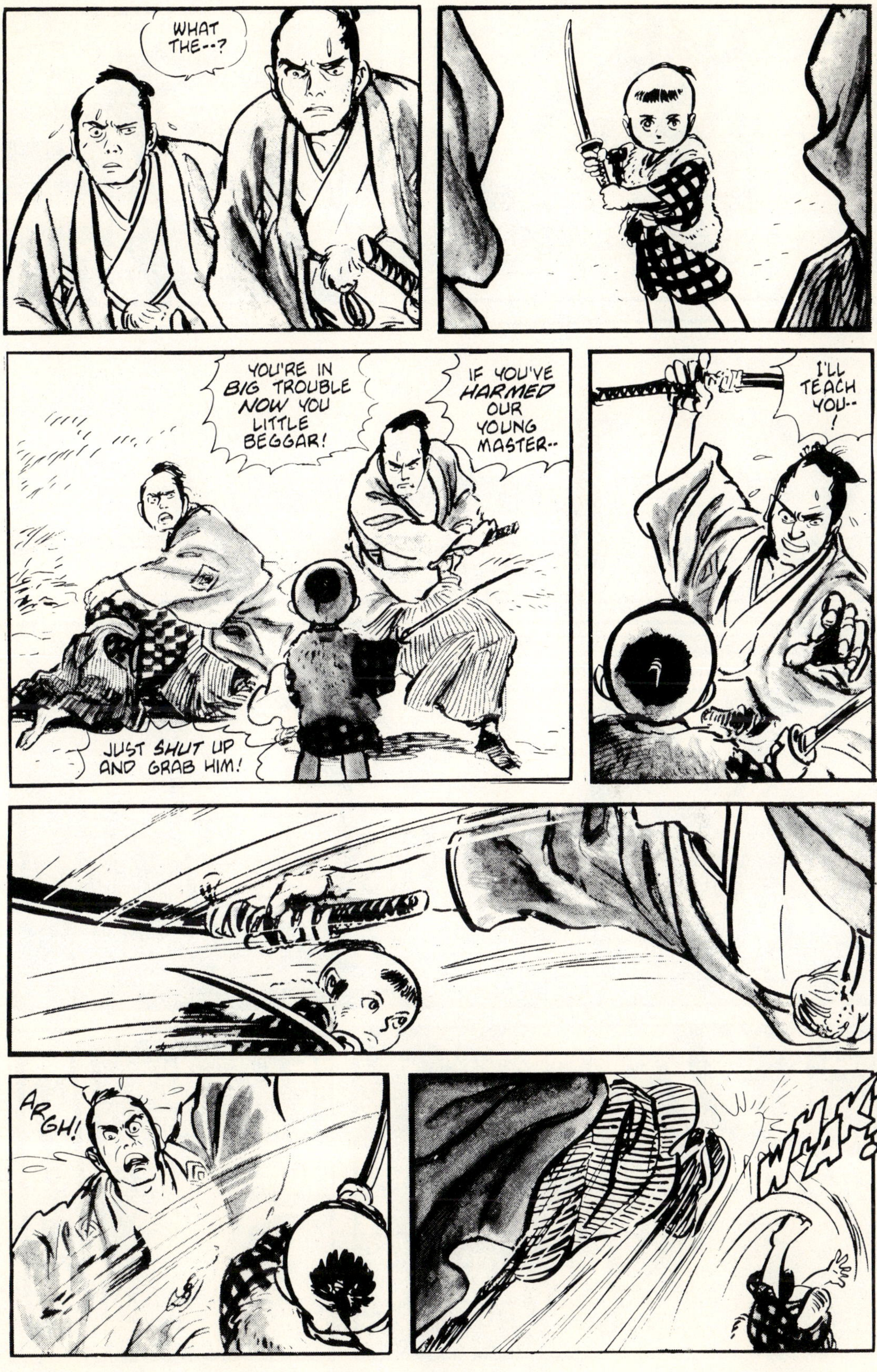
WHAT THE--?
YOU'RE IN BIG TROUBLE NOW YOU LITTLE BEGGAR!
IF YOU'VE HARMED OUR YOUNG MASTER--
JUST SHUT UP AND GRAB HIM!
I'LL TEACH YOU--!
ARGH!
WHAK!

WHUMP
buh-huh-WAAAA!
I'M B-B-BLEEDING!
A "MAID-MERCHANT" AND HIS CHARGES APPROACH A NOBLE ESTATE.
TAKIZAWA FAMILY. SERVANT'S ENTRANCE.
滝澤家通用門

FOR YOUR INSPECTION HOUSEKEEPER, I SUBMIT THESE THREE YOUTHFUL CANDIDATES. I ASSURE YOU THEY ARE HEALTHY, DILIGENT, AND...

ENOUGH, GET STARTED.
THE LOWEST RANKING MAID IN A HOUSE WAS ALWAYS CALLED OSUE, "THE LAST".
WHENEVER A NEW OSUE WAS HIRED...
SEVERAL PROSPECTS WOULD BE TESTED FOR DEX-TERITY.

*TOFU- SOYBEAN CURD.

HURRY! THIS IS AN EMERGENCY!
I'M BLEEDING!
IT'S THE YOUNG MASTER.
CALL THE DOCTOR! HURRY!
huh-WAAAH!
WHAT'S ALL THIS FUSS?
OH! YOUNG MASTER!
SHINNOSUKE! WHAT HAPPENED?

WAAA!
BA-WAAAA!
hic-hic-SNIFF--
SHINNOSUKE! PULL YOURSELF TOGETHER!
WAH-WA-hic-WAH-hic!
NO SAMURAI CHILD EVER CRIES OVER A LITTLE CUT LIKE THAT. YOU'RE CARRYING ON LIKE A GIRL!
HOW CAN WE EVER APOLOGIZE, YOUR LADYSHIP!
HE WAS RIGHT AT OUR SIDE--HOW COULD THIS HAPPEN?

WELL, THERE'S NO NEED TO WORRY. IT'S ONLY A SHALLOW WOUND. IT WILL HEAL SOON.
WHEW!
LATER.
SMAK!
SLAP!
WHAK!
SMAK!
WHAK!
WHAT THE-- NO ONE TAKES THIS KIND OF PUNISHMENT SO CALMLY! HE SHOWS NO FEAR, NO PAIN... HE HASN'T SHED A TEAR! IT GIVES ME THE CREEPS!
HE'S THE STRANGEST LITTLE BRAT I'VE EVER SEEN!
DON'T BE RIDICULOUS! IT'S MERELY THAT REBELLIOUS ATTITUDE YOU FIND AMONG THE LOWER CLASSES. NOW WHAT SHALL WE DO WITH HIM?

WHAT ABOUT HIS PARENTS? THEY SHOULD TAKE RESPONSIBLITY FOR THIS!
WHAT DO YOU SUGGEST, YOUR LADY-SHIP?
I WISH I KNEW! OH, WHAT A HORRID CHILD!
JUST LEAVE HIM TO ME...
I'LL MAKE THE LITTLE WRETCH TALK!
YOU LITTLE BEAST! I'LL MAKE YOU SCREAM FOR HURTING OUR PRECIOUS SIRE!

TELL US WHO YOU ARE OR I'LL STAB YOU! I MEAN IT!
I'LL HURT YOU! I'LL MAKE YOU BLEED!
SPITEFUL LITTLE BRAT!
WAIT!
OH... MASTER. WELCOME HOME.
SOMETHING TERRIBLE HAS HAPPENED...

I'VE HEARD ALL THE DETAILS, AND YET...
WHAT IS IT?
THOSE EYES...
LIKE LIFE-DEATH EYES. AS THOUGH HE'D WITNESSED COUNTLESS SCENES OF CARNAGE!
LIFE-DEATH EYES?
YES, BETWEEN LIFE AND DEATH. AN ASSASSIN'S EYES, ABLE TO PLACE HIS HEART IN A STATE OF UTTER SELFLESSNESS.
IT'S CHILLING! THESE PURE, FLAWLESS EYES FILL ME WITH SUCH FEAR...
IT'S IMPOSSIBLE!
I'D LIKE TO THINK SO... BUT THE GLEAM IN THIS CHILD'S EYES UNNERVES ME. THEY LOOK STRAIGHT INTO MY SOUL.

NOW THAT YOU MENTION IT--WHEN THE BRAT ATTACKED THE YOUNG MASTER HE HAD THAT LOOK.
AND HIS STRANGE FIGHTING STANCE..
WHAT !?
WHAT WAS THIS STANCE?
OH, GOD, NO!
SUIO-STYLE ZANBATO.
IS IT POSSIBLE? IS THIS...
HURRY! LOCK THE CHILD IN THE WAREHOUSE. ALLOW HIM NO FOOD OR WATER.
WHY? WHAT'S GOING ON?

*HAN--PROVINCE.

*METSUKE--WATCHMAN.

ELSEWHERE.

BASH!
SLASH!

CLANG!
CHING!
HA HA HA HA HA HA HA
HA HA HA HA HA
HA HA HA HA HA

UGH...
...ARGH...
MY FEVER MUST BE BREAKING... THIS LOOKS LIKE A ROAD-SIDE SHRINE...
HOW LONG HAVE I BEEN HERE?

SUCH NIGHTMARES! I DREAMED I WAS PURSUED BY THE DEMONS OF HELL. IS IT A SIGN THAT MY FEVER HAS PASSED--
OR THAT DEATH IS NEAR?
UNGH!
PANT PANT

PUFF
PUFF
CHOK!
CHOK!
SKREE
SREAK

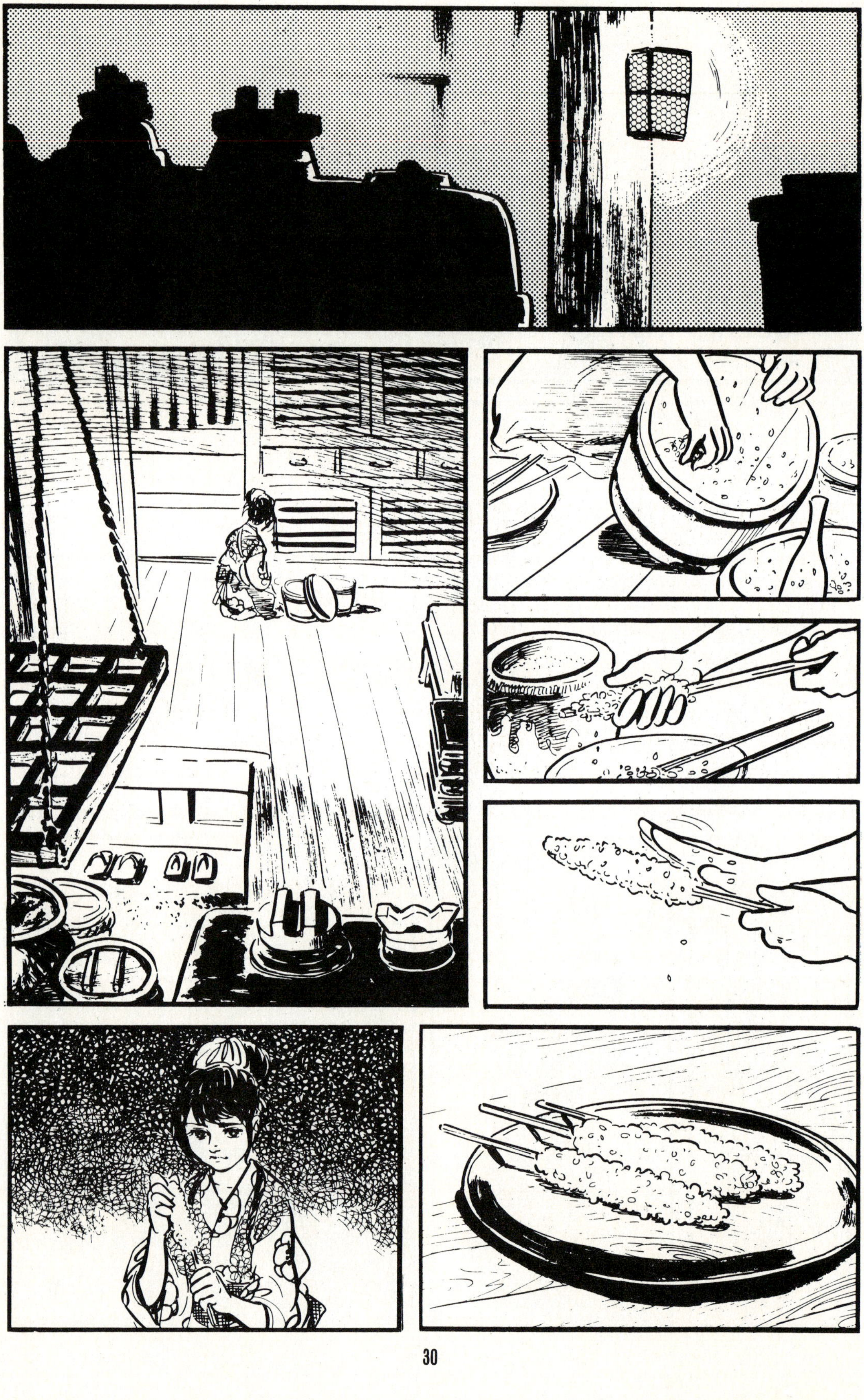

FUMP!

PLINK
HOW CAN THEY BE SO CRUEL TO A POOR LITTLE THING LIKE YOU?
YOU MUST BE AWFUL HUNGRY. HERE, TAKE THESE RICE STICKS.
THE SALT MAKES THEM TASTE BETTER. WAIT A MINUTE.
IT'LL MAKE YOU THIRSTY. HERE'S SOME SNOW.
THANKS, SIS.

WHERE'S YOUR MOMMY AND DADDY?
IF YOU TELL ME WHERE THEY ARE, I'LL GO GET THEM.
I THOUGHT YOU WERE ON YOUR OWN... I JUST HAD A FEELING.
WHEN I SAW YOU AT THE RIVER YOU LOOKED SO *LONELY*. ME TOO. I'M ALL ALONE.
I'LL BE BACK LATER WITH MORE. DON'T CRY, OKAY? I WON'T ABANDON YOU.
MMM.

HOW STRANGE!
THREE DAYS AND HE SHOWS NO SIGN OF WEAKENING.
NO FEAR, NO TEARS, NO CALL FOR HELP...
HOW CAN HE GO WITHOUT FOOD OR WATER? HMMM...
A-HA!
FOOT PRINTS...
SO!

EEEEK!
COME ON-- TALK, DAMN YOU!
BASH!
HARDER! SHOW NO MERCY!
WHY DID YOU COME TO THIS HOUSEHOLD?
WHAT IS YOUR RELATION TO THE CHILD?
BASH! BASH!

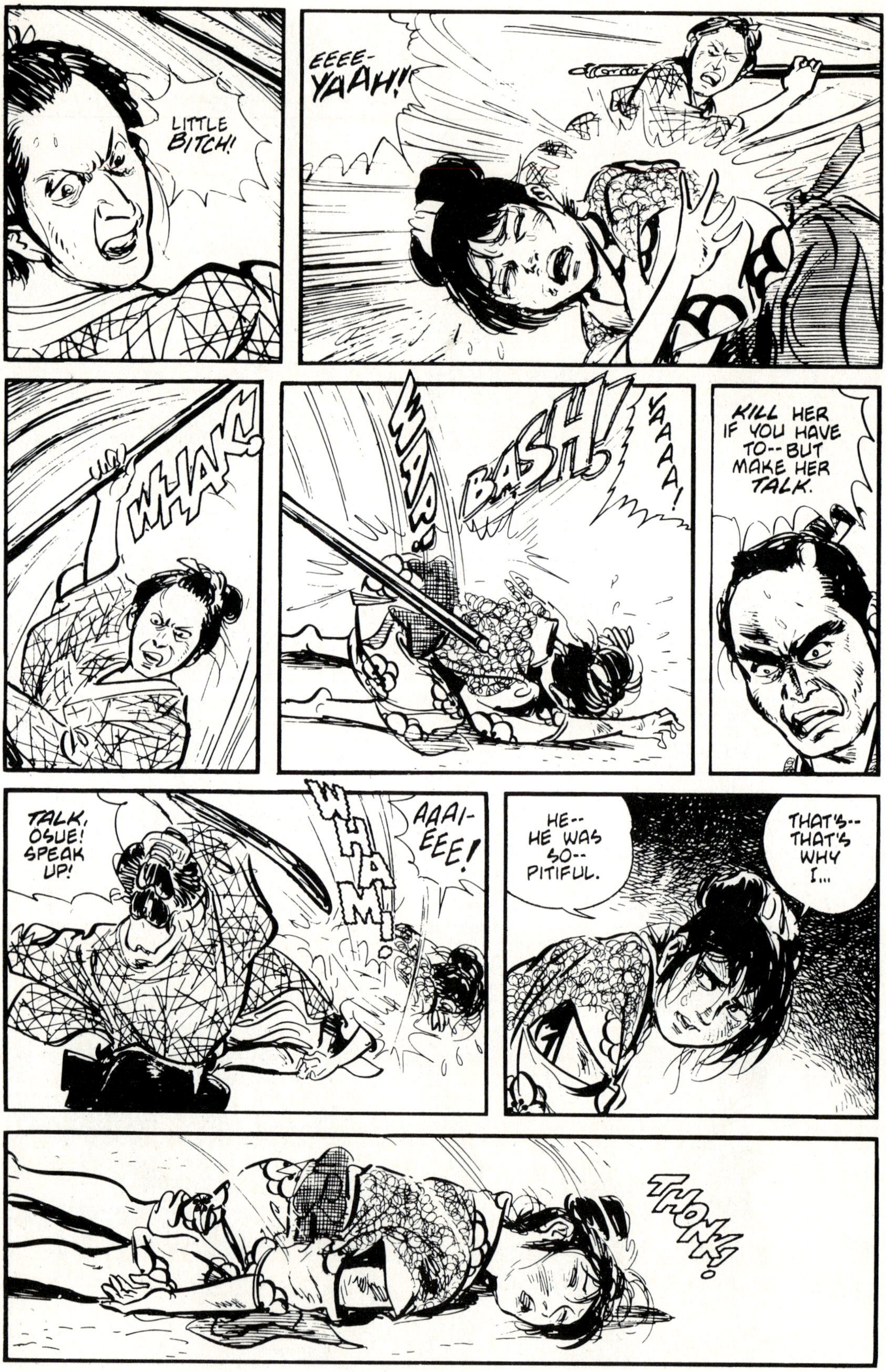
LITTLE BITCH!
EEEE-YAAH!
WHAK!
WARP!
BASH!
YAAAAA!
KILL HER IF YOU HAVE TO--BUT MAKE HER TALK.
TALK, OSUE! SPEAK UP!
WHAM!
AAAI-EEEE!
HE--HE WAS SO--PITIFUL.
THAT'S--THAT'S WHY I...
THONK!

THE TAKIZAWA GUARD HOUSE.
THE ASSASSIN KNOWN AS THE LONE WOLF WILL STOP AT NOTHING!
HE DELIBERATELY USED HIS SON TO INJURE SHINNOSUKE, AND LET US CAPTURE THE CHILD. THEN HE SENT THAT GIRL AS AN OSUE TO KEEP AN EYE ON HIM.
ALL EVIDENCE SHOWS THAT I AM HIS TARGET. ME-- THE HAN METSUKE!
WE CAN'T WAIT A SECOND! IF WE WAIT FOR HIM TO COME TO US, WE'VE LOST THE ADVANTAGE. HUNT HIM DOWN! HE MUST BE CLOSE BY!
DON'T REST UNTIL WE FIND THE LONE WOLF!

SLOOSH
THUD
SIS!
SIS!
R-RUN AWAY...!
UHN...
THUD

HE SAID "SIS." I HEARD HIM.
JUST AS I SUSPECTED!
BUT WHO WOULD HAVE THOUGHT THAT THEY WERE BROTHER AND SISTER?

DASH
WHA--?
OH!

THUNK!
GYAAAH!
YOU BRAT!
GET HIM!
WAIT!
LET HIM ESCAPE-- AND THEN FOLLOW HIM.
YES, SIR!

HE'LL RUN TO THE PAPA-WOLF! THIS IS THE CHANCE WE'VE BEEN WAITING FOR!
DON'T GET CARELESS JUST BECAUSE HE'S A CHILD! YOU'VE SEEN HOW FIERCE HE IS!
YES, SIR!
AS LONG AS THE GIRL IS IN OUR HANDS WE HAVE AN EDGE.
WHO'D IMAGINE THAT THE LONE WOLF HAD TWO CHILDREN? ANOTHER SURPRISE...
SIS!
SIS!

PANT
PANT
CLICK
DAIGORO! I DON'T KNOW WHAT KIND OF TROUBLE YOU'VE GOTTEN INTO--BUT ARE YOU SURE YOU CAN FINISH IT ALONE!

THIS IS IT!
YEAH.
I KNEW IT!
THAT'S HIM!

I DON'T KNOW WHAT'S GOING ON HERE...
AND IT WOULD SEEM THE TIME FOR *TALK* HAS PASSED.
WOOOSH!
GYAAAH!

SLAP!
UNGH!

UNGH...
K-CHINK!
OOOF!
THUNK!
WE'VE FOUND HIM!
SO, HE IS HERE!
YES, THE LONE WOLF AND CUB WITHOUT A DOUBT! BY A SHRINE ON THE RIVER BANK!

SIS!

ARE YOU THE ONES KNOWN AS LONE WOLF AND CUB?
MY NAME'S UNIMPORTANT. I'M ONLY A PASSING TRAVELLER.
DON'T GIVE ME THAT! WE'VE UNCOVERED YOUR PLOT!
YOU WON'T SLIP THROUGH MY HANDS NOW!

AAAAH...
IF YOU DON'T TALK THE GIRL DIES!
TALK!
WHO HIRED YOU? WHO HAVE YOU COME TO MURDER?
IF YOU VALUE YOUR DAUGHTER'S LIFE, DROP YOUR SWORD!
SIS!
WHY DOES THE SNOW FALL...
PEOPLE SHIVER, NOT KNOWING THE REASON...
THE SNOW DOESN'T CARE THAT IT CHILLS THE HEARTS OF MEN.
IT'S INEVITABLE.
THUMP
HA HA HA! I THOUGHT SO! SHE IS YOUR CHILD!

WOOSH!
SUDDENLY, HIDDEN SPEARS SPRING FROM DAIGORO'S BABY CART...
GAH! K-K-K-!
SPLUSSSSH!
WHA..?

CHOP!
YAAA!
CH-KLANG!

ZAASH!

THE END

NEXT MONTH

The Lone Wolf has chosen the assassin's road; but can he truly transcend himself and become the perfect assassin? Is it possible for him to reach the state of "Mu" — to feel nothing? "When you meet the Buddha, kill the Buddha." These words echo in Itto Ogami's mind when he is hired to kill a wise and benevolent priest who shows him the road to "The Gateless Barrier."

来月

AFTERWORD

For those of you, like me, who were a tad confused by the last few pages of this issue, some additional explanation might be helpful.

First of all, the young maid was *not* Itto Ogami's daughter. Then why did Daigoro call her "sis?" In Japan it is quite common to refer to complete strangers as if they were members of your immediate family. The Japanese word for "uncle" is something of a generic term for any old man. If you were Japanese and saw an old lady laden with parcels and offered to give her a hand, you might say, "Here, Auntie, let me help you with those." Similarly, "sis" might refer to any young woman. Daigoro didn't know her name; so he just called her "sis."

"Okay, smarty-pants," you're probably thinking, "then why did everyone think she was Daigoro's sister and, consequently, Ogami's daughter?"

Well, that's a little trickier. But try to picture yourself as a local feudal land baron in a country rife with political intrigue, where the simplest way to eliminate your political rivals was to hire an assassin to go whack them. Naturally, you're going to assume that *your* rivals have similar plans for your future, and you're likely to see convoluted plots where none exist. In other words, you might be a little paranoid. Such was the world of the Tokugawa Shogunate.

So as soon as they discovered that Itto Ogami, the dreaded assassin, was in their province, they naturally assumed he was there to kill some important personage in the local hierarchy. They thought he used his son Daigoro to gain entry to the estate — and they thought the new maid must be Ogami's daughter since she showed compassion for Daigoro. They were wrong on all three counts. Just a simple mistake. A deadly one.

後文

Okay. That's the easy stuff. Now what about the *deus ex machina* on page 52? "Suddenly, hidden spears spring from Daigoro's baby cart." Ha! Come on! Who is going to believe that?

The baby cart is an integral part of Lone Wolf and Cub. In fact, the series is frequently referred to as "The Baby Cart Assassin." In one of the numerous movies based on the series, *Lightning Swords of Death*, the cart possesses not only hidden spears, but a concealed gattling gun (a primitive machine gun) as well! One of these issues we'll have to whip up a schematic diagram of the cart. But for now just think of it as the Japanese equivalent of James Bond's Astin-Martin in the movie version of *Goldfinger*.

Why don't they explain that somewhere in the series? Well, to tell you the truth, I don't have an answer for that one right now. I could just cop-out and say "Because Japanese comics are different from American comics," but I won't. Instead, I'll just say that this series is over 9,000 pages long, and I haven't actually read all of them yet since most of them are still only in Japanese; so maybe they *do* explain the baby cart somewhere down the line. I know it's not the best explanation in the world, but at 64 pages of story and art per month, I've got almost twelve years to change it!

— *Rick Oliver*

THE FIRST CHOICE...

AMERICAN FLAGG!
BADGER
CORUM
DREADSTAR
DYNAMO JOE
ELRIC
EVANGELINE
GRIMJACK
HAWKMOON
JON SABLE, FREELANCE
LONE WOLF AND CUB
NEXUS
SHATTER
WHISPER

<u>COMING SOON:</u>
PSYCHOBLAST

...THE BEST CHOICE.

Make the First Choice...the *Best* Choice
Subscribe now! Never miss a single issue!
Don't talk with your mouth full!

Yes! I want a 12 issue subscription to:

Only $15.00!
☐ American Flagg!
☐ Dynamo Joe
☐ Grimjack
☐ Whisper
($17 in Canada, $32 foreign rate)

Only $21.00!
☐ Badger
☐ Corum
☐ Dreadstar
☐ Evangeline
☐ Elric
☐ Hawkmoon
☐ Jon Sable
☐ Nexus
☐ Shatter
($23 in Canada, $40 foreign rate)

Only $23.00!
☐ Lone Wolf and Cub
(U.S. subscription only)

Name______________________________
Address____________________________
City_______________________________
State_______________Zip_______________

Make checks payable to:
First Comics Publishing
435 N. La Salle St.
Chicago, IL 60610

FIRST COMICS ®
COUNT ON US.
TM & © 1987 FIRST COMICS, INC.

All payments in U.S. funds. Offer expires June 30, 1987.